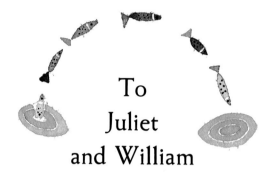

To
Juliet
and William

First North American Edition 1993
First published in Great Britain in 1992 by ABC, All Books for Children

ISBN 0-316-58405-3
Library of Congress Catalog Card Number 92-53215
Library of Congress Cataloging-in-Publication information is available.

10 9 8 7 6 5 4 3 2 1

Published simultaneously in Canada
by Little, Brown & Company (Canada) Limited

Printed in Singapore

A Spider
and a Pig

Carol Morley

Little, Brown and Company

Boston Toronto London

In the remote sea of Sasparilla on the other side of the world is a little island called Silkythread.

Silkythread is named after its spiders, who spin beautiful webs. It is not named after its truffles, mushrooms that taste delicious but, unfortunately, are also very smelly.

On this island a daughter
was born to the Mayor and his wife,
who had longed for a child for many
years. Clarissa was very tiny
and frail, and in order to
clothe her in the softest
garments, the Mayor asked
every spider on the island
(and there were lots) to spin
their finest silk and weave
it into bedclothes.

The Mayor was so delighted
with the results that he granted a
special day for the spiders to spin,
a day when no one could touch the
silky webs: no children could waggle
sticks in them, and no dogs could run
through them. Only Celia, the
smallest spider, did not
spin because she was
too young. So she just
watched, perched on
the head of her best
friend, Julius the pig.

Now, pigs are famous for
their truffle-hunting noses, and
of all the pigs on the island, Julius
had the very best nose. He knew every
nook and cranny of the forest and could
always sniff out the biggest truffles.

Suddenly, the sky grew black and lightning crashed. Rain pelted down, the wind whistled, and everything flew through the air. Spiders got tangled in their webs, roofs tore off buildings, and people were swept off their feet. Celia was blown into the village pond, where she struggled to stay afloat on an oak leaf.

Then, in one horrifying gust, the wind
swept into baby Clarissa's room, gathered
her up, and blew her out the window,
high across the village, and
into the forest, where she
disappeared from view.

When the wind
stopped, Julius leapt
into the pond to
save Celia.

He splashed and snorted and
almost drowned before he struggled
out with Celia on his snout.

The island was in a terrible state. The spiders were caught in their webs. Buildings and people and animals were everywhere.

But, worst of all, Clarissa was nowhere
to be found. The Mayor and his wife
were beside themselves with worry and
asked everyone to help search for her.

Everyone searched.
Spiders looked under
every floorboard.

Butchers and bakers, horses and
hounds, children and their nurses looked
down every chimney. Everyone hunted
except Julius, who had caught a cold, so
he could not smell, and Celia, whose
legs were wobbly. But Clarissa
had simply disappeared.

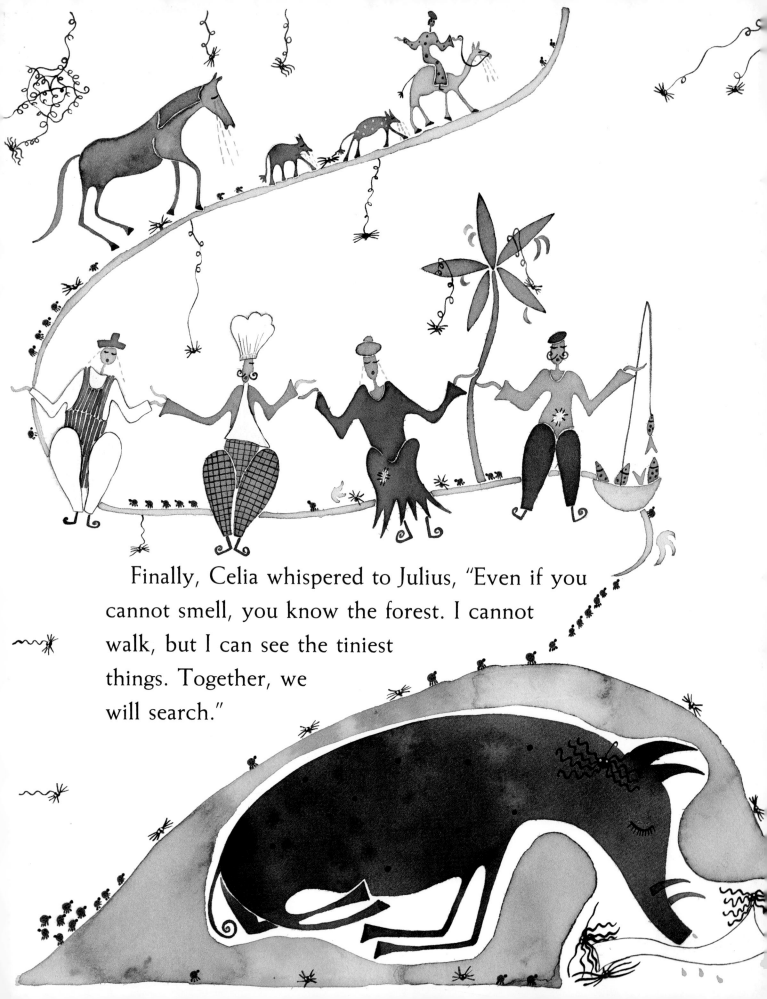

Finally, Celia whispered to Julius, "Even if you cannot smell, you know the forest. I cannot walk, but I can see the tiniest things. Together, we will search."

The villagers
shook their heads

as a spider who
could not walk

and a pig who
could not smell

set off.

They looked under every toadstool and behind every
tree until at last Celia said, "Up there, off that branch!"
Julius looked but could see nothing, for it was only
a wisp of web, too small for his piggy eyes.

Celia climbed Julius's ear, pulled herself
up the thread, and followed it onto a
broad tree leaf. There was little
Clarissa, nestled in quite warm
and dry and fast asleep.

When Julius and Celia returned to the village
with Clarissa, they were greeted with a cheering
welcome and a special feast. Even the spiders
clapped with all their legs.

"What do I smell?" cried Julius.
"Your cold must be better," laughed Celia.

And everyone on Silkythread sat down
to enjoy truffle soup.